TO _____

Disney's
SMALL WORLD LIBRARY
GOOFY ON SAFARI
An Adventure in Kenya

GROLIER ENTERPRISES INC.
DANBURY, CONNECTICUT

© The Walt Disney Company. All rights reserved.
Printed in the United States of America.
Developed by The Walt Disney Company in conjunction with Nancy Hall, Inc.
ISBN: 0-7172-8225-2

It was another busy day in Nairobi, Kenya's bustling capital city. So many different kinds of people! So many languages to hear! So many things to see and do!

Minnie, Clarabelle, and Goofy had come to Africa to go on a wildlife safari. Since they had only one day to spend in Nairobi, they decided to make the most of it. They had already toured the National Museum and visited a local art gallery.

Afterwards, they decided to go to an open-air market. While Minnie and Clarabelle were admiring some beautiful handmade baskets, Goofy made friends with a boy named Sekento from the Masai tribe.

Sekento had come to the market to buy a cowbell.
"This year I have my own herd to take care of," he
told Goofy proudly. "One of my calves, Songori, has been
straying from the flock and into the Masai Mara game
park. Maybe this bell will help me keep better track of
her."

"We're going to the Masai Mara game park tomorrow to see the animals," said Goofy.

"Then you must come visit me, too," declared Sekento. "My home is very near the game park."

Sekento wrote down the dircctions to his village, and Goofy put them in his pocket.

"Ole sere," said Sekento. "That means, 'Go in peace.' "

"Ole sere," repeated Goofy. "See you tomorrow!" he added, waving good-bye.

Minnie, Clarabelle, and Goofy arrived at the game park just as it was getting dark. They had dinner around the campfire and then it was time for bed.

Goofy was about to doze off when he heard all sorts of strange noises. First, a lion roared a ferocious warning. Then, when he heard a water buffalo bellow to its mate, Goofy sprang out of his sleeping bag.

"Those animals sound scary!" he cried. Goofy covered his ears to block out the night noises, but it was no use. "This safari stuff doesn't seem like so much fun now," he thought.

"Ha, ha, ha!" laughed a hyena.

"Be quiet," grumbled Goofy, pulling his pillow over his head. He tossed and turned for the rest of the night, trying to decide whether or not to go on the tour the next day. By morning he had made up his mind.

"I'm not going with you," Goofy told Minnie and Clarabelle over breakfast. "I didn't get much sleep last night," he yawned. "I think I'll just spend the day bird-watching."

"But then you won't get to see all the animals," said Clarabelle. "That's why we came to Africa, remember?"

"I heard enough of the animals last night!" thought Goofy. "I've decided to go bird-watching around the campground instead," he said aloud.

Just then a tour guide pulled up in his mini-van.
Goofy watched as Clarabelle and Minnie climbed aboard.
"Have a good time!" he called.
The tour guide turned to Goofy. "Don't wander too far
from camp," he warned.
"I sure won't!" said Goofy.

It was a beautiful morning. Wherever Minnie and
Clarabelle looked around the countryside, there was
something new to see. The tour guide stopped when they
came to a large umbrella thorn tree. Underneath it, a
family of cheetah cubs played with each other like a litter
of kittens.

"Look in the tree," said the guide, pointing. There,
balanced on a tree limb, a mother cheetah watched over
the babies.

A while later a tiny creature darted in front of them.
"Is that a baby deer?" asked Minnie.

"No," answered the guide. "It's not a baby at all. It's a
full grown dik-dik, which is the smallest antelope in the
world."

Meanwhile, Goofy was looking for a nice spot to begin bird-watching. He had packed himself a picnic lunch and was about to spread his blanket, when a flash of rainbow-colored feathers fluttered past him and landed on a nearby branch.

"What luck!" cried Goofy. "That is the most beautiful bird I've ever seen!"

He quickly leafed through his field guide until he came to the right page: "The superb starling is one of Kenya's most spectacular birds," he read.

Goofy was almost ready to take the bird's picture when it flew to another tree. He followed it closely as it flitted from one spot to another until, without knowing it, Goofy wandered right into the game reserve!

Goofy found a comfortable spot and sat down on a nice big rock to have his lunch. He was about to bite into his sandwich when another brightly colored bird caught his attention.

"I just love bird-watching!" he said, reaching for his
field guide. "That's a golden-backed weaver," he read.

He picked up his camera, but before he could focus it,
the weaver flew away.

"Come back!" cried Goofy, forgetting all about his
lunch. He threw down his sandwich and raced after the
tiny bird.

"Here, birdie," called Goofy. He chased the little bird from tree to tree, never taking his eyes off it—not even when an elephant sprayed him with a trunkful of water!

"Gawrsh!" he cried. "I needed that. Nothing like a little shower to cool a guy off!"

Goofy followed the weaver through a field of tall grass.
"I'm sure glad there aren't any wild animals around
here to worry about!" he said happily.

The weaver finally landed. Goofy inched toward it on tiptoe, so as not to disturb it. But when he got closer he noticed that the bird had perched on the head of a small animal. Goofy moved a little closer.

"Well, I'll be!" he muttered. "It's a baby cow!"

Then Goofy saw the cowbell tied around the animal's neck.

"It must be Sekento's calf!" he said.

Goofy reached into his pocket and took out the directions to Sekento's village. Then, leading the calf by its rope, he went to find Sekento.

Sekento was delighted to see Goofy with the baby calf.
"Songori!" cried Sekento, hugging the calf tightly. "I
thought I would never see you again! You shouldn't roll
in the mud," he scolded. "Some of it must have clogged
your bell. See, it doesn't even ring anymore!"

Then, turning to Goofy, he said warmly, "How can I
ever thank you, my friend?"

"Gawrsh!" replied Goofy. "It wasn't any trouble at all."

"Tomorrow my people are planning a big celebration to welcome the rainy season," said Sekento. "I would be honored if you and your friends would come."

"That sure sounds like fun," said Goofy. "We'll be there!"

Goofy went back the way he came. He wondered why anybody would have a party just because it was going to rain.

"But a party is a party," he thought, and he began to whistle a happy tune.

Before long, he heard a horn toot, and then he saw a mini-van about to pass him.

"Can that be Goofy?" cried Minnie in disbelief.

The guide brought the mini-van to a screeching halt. "Get in," he ordered Goofy. "Hurry!"

"You'll never believe the day I had!" said Goofy as he climbed aboard the mini-van. "I found Sekento's calf, and Sekento invited me to a party. Want to go?"

"Sure!" chorused Minnie and Clarabelle.

But the guide still looked angry. "You were supposed to stay close to the camp, where it's safe," he said to Goofy. "Don't you know there are dangerous wild animals around here?"

"Here?" said Goofy in surprise. "I've been out here all day, and the only animal I've seen is Sekento's calf."

"Then you were very lucky," replied the guide. "Do you see that Cape buffalo over there? It just happens to be one of the most dangerous animals on the African plain!"

"Gawrsh!" said Goofy. "I didn't know that bird-watching could be so risky!"

The next day the guide drove everyone to the Masai village. Sekento was waiting for them.

"The old people of our village say it will rain today," he said, gazing up at the dark clouds. "They have a special way of telling these things, and they are almost never wrong. Besides, I think you will bring us good luck," he added. "After all, Goofy found Songori for me."

Sekento presented each of his new friends with a beautiful necklace. Then he taught them all a special Masai song and dance.

Sekento sang a song about how the rain would fill the streams and make the plains turn green with grass. The song told about how fat and healthy the cattle would become when they had feasted on the new grass.

Just then a drop of water fell on Goofy's nose.

"What was that?" asked Goofy.

"Rain!" cried Sekento, turning his palms up to catch the drops.

Soon the rain was falling steadily, and everyone began
to cheer. Goofy and his friends joined the Masai in a
dance of thanksgiving.

"This is going to be a wonderful year for my people!"
laughed Sekento. "I knew you would bring us luck!"

"Gawrsh!" said Goofy. "I guess I'm even luckier than I
thought!"

Did You Know...?

There are many different customs and places that make each country special. Do you remember some of the things below from the story?

The Masai are one of many different groups of people living in Kenya. Each group, or tribe, has its own language, culture, and way of life. But they also share an official national language, Kiswahili (Kee-swah-hee-lee), so tribes can communicate with each other.

The cheetah is the fastest animal on earth. It can run as fast as seventy miles per hour.

Cattle are very important to the Masai tribe. According to one of their legends, all the world's cattle once belonged to them. The wealth of a Masai family is measured by the number of cattle it owns.

The dik-dik is the world's smallest antelope. It stands only fifteen inches high at the shoulder. Many Kenyans have dik-diks as pets.

Kenyans have a special dance for every occasion, such as the birth of a child or a wedding. Many dancers wear colorful headdresses and painted masks that look like animals or birds. On national holidays, tribes compete against each other in dance contests.

Kenyan musicians play many unusual instruments. One is called a thumb piano or *mbira* (em-beer-ah). It is a box containing flat strips of metal that are plucked by the player's thumbs to make musical notes.

People come to Kenya's open-air markets to buy, sell, and trade food and goods. The markets are also a great place to meet friends and exchange news.

Mt. Kenya is the second tallest mountain in Africa. Although it lies close to the hot regions near the equator, it is snow-covered all year long. Climbers can tell their friends they had a snowball fight near the equator!

"Tutaonana!" (Too-tah-OH-nah-nah) means "See you soon!" in Kiswahili.